D1139184

Archie's UNBELIEVABLY Freaky Week

www.davidficklingbooks.co.uk

Also by Andrew Norriss

I Don't Believe It, Archie!
Aquila
Aquila 2
Ctrl-Z
The Portal
The Unluckiest Boy in the World
The Touchstone
Bernard's Watch
Matt's Million
Woof! A Twist in the Tale
Woof! The Tale Gets Longer
Woof! The Tale Wags On

Archie's UNBELIEVABLY Freaky Week

ANDREW NORRISS

ILLUSTRATED BY Hannah Shaw

David Fickling Books

OXFORD · NEW YORK

31 Beaumont Street
Oxford OX1 2NP, UK

ARCHIE'S UNBELIEVABLE FREAKY WEEK
A DAVID FICKLING BOOK ISBN 978-0-857-56011-7
Published in Great Britain by David Fickling Books,
a division of Random House Children's Publishers UK
A Random House Group Company

This edition published 2012
Text copyright © Andrew Norriss, 2012
Illustrations copyright © Hannah Shaw, 2012

The Random House Group Limited supports the Forest Stewardship
CouncilThe Random House Group Limited supports The Forest Stewardship Council
(FSC®), the leading international forest certification organisation. Our books
carrying the FSC label are printed on FSC® certified paper. FSC is the only for
est certification scheme endorsed by the leading environmental organisations,
including Greenpeace. Our paper procurement policy can be found at
www.randomhouse.co.uk/environment

Set in 13/18pt Baskerville

DAVID FICKLING BOOKS
31 Beaumont Street, Oxford, OX1 2NP

www.**kids**at**randomhouse**.co.uk
www.**totallyrandombooks**.co.uk
www.randomhouse.co.uk

Addresses for companies within The Random House Group Limited can be found at:
www.randomhouse.co.uk/offices.htm

THE RANDOM HOUSE GROUP Limited Reg. No. 954009

A CIP catalogue record for this book is available from the British Library.

Printed and bound in Great Britain by Clays Ltd, St Ives plc

This book is dedicated to all those teachers who cope with the Archies in their classes with endless patience, kindness, and only the occasional hissy fit . . .

1. On Monday . . .

On Monday, when Archie got to school, he found the body of Mrs Boyd, the school cook, lying in the car park.

'Har hoo hor hi?' he asked. He was trying to say *Are you all right?* but he had been to the dentist that morning and the injection he had been given made it difficult to talk.

'Oh, thank goodness!' said Mrs Boyd, when she saw him. 'I've been shouting for nearly an hour, but nobody heard. I've got my arm stuck in this drain.'

She explained that on her way into school, she had dropped her car keys. 'They fell through the grating,' she said, 'so I put my arm down to get them back, but now it's stuck. Could you go and tell someone?'

'Hess, hohorse,' said Archie, meaning *Yes, of course*.

'And could you take my bag to the kitchens?' said Mrs Boyd. 'It's got today's menu in it and if they don't have it soon, nobody'll get any lunch.'

'Hohay,' said Archie, meaning *OK*, and he picked up the bag and ran into school.

'Morning, Archie!' said the school secretary, as she buzzed the door to let him in. 'How did you get on at the dentist?'

'Hissis Hoy,' said Archie. 'His hin ha harhar.' He was trying to say *Mrs Boyd is in the car park*, but that was the best he could manage.

'Goodness!' The secretary smiled. 'You're not going to be able to talk properly for hours, are you!'

'Hissis Hoy . . .' Archie tried again, '. . . his hin ha—'

'I'm sorry, I can't understand a word you're saying, but wait there. Mr Gunn wants to talk to you.' The secretary came out from behind her desk. 'He's outside somewhere, but he wants to tell you about your new class teacher. I'll see if I can find him.'

'Hees,' said Archie. 'Hoo ha hoo hissen.'

He meant *Please, you have to listen*, but the secretary had already gone.

Archie wasn't sure what to do. He had to

tell someone about Mrs Boyd, but if no one could understand what he was saying, it wasn't going to be easy.

Then he had an idea.

Taking an exercise book from his bag, he tore out a page and wrote: *Mrs Boyd is in the car park, with her arm stuck down a drain.*

All he had to do now was decide who he should give the message to. He could wait for the secretary to come back with the Head Teacher, but Archie thought it might be quicker if he took it to the kitchens. Mrs Boyd had asked him to take the menu there, so he could deliver her bag and the message at the same time.

On his way to the kitchens, however, walking past the main staircase, Archie was stopped by a loud voice.

'I don't believe it!' it said. 'It's you, isn't it!'

Archie looked up to see a woman on the stairs above him. She had huge muscles in her arms and legs, a tattoo around her neck, and an angry look on her face.

'You're the boy who mugged that woman in the car park, aren't you?' she said, 'and then stole her bag!'

'Ho! Ho, ho!' said Archie. He was trying to say *No! No, no!* but it came out sounding a bit like Father Christmas.

'Yes, you did! I saw you from my classroom window!'

'Ho!' said Archie. 'Hi hidden hoo hennyhing.' He held out the note he had written about Mrs Boyd. 'Here!' he said. 'Heed hiss!'

The woman with the tattoo took the note, read it, and her eyes narrowed.

'Are you mad?' she demanded.

It wasn't quite the response Archie had been expecting. The woman obviously didn't believe what he had written about Mrs Boyd, so he held up the bag the cook had given him.

'He haive he her hag,' he said. He was trying to say *She gave me her bag* and, as a way of showing why he had been given it, he reached inside the bag for the menu. It was underneath a large kitchen knife so he took that out first . . .

. . . And the next thing he knew, the woman with the tattoo had leaped down the last few stairs, grabbed his arm with one hand, his shirt collar with the other, and sent him somersaulting through the air. He landed with a thud on the hall floor, and found the woman with the tattoo was sitting on his chest.

Archie was used to odd things happening to him – they happened to him every day – but all this was odder than usual, even for him.

'I don't believe it!' said a voice. 'Miss Hurrell? What are you doing?'

To Archie's relief, Mr Gunn, the Head Teacher, was running down the corridor towards them, the secretary hurrying along behind him.

'He came at me with a knife,' said the woman with the tattoo. 'I had no choice.'

'Oh, please!' said Mr Gunn. 'This is Archie, the boy I told you about! For goodness sake get up and let him breathe.'

The woman with the tattoo did as she was told, and Mr Gunn asked Archie if he was all right.

'Ho,' said Archie.

'He came at me with a knife,' the woman with the tattoo repeated. 'He said he wanted to kill me!'

'Kill you?' said Mr Gunn. 'What are you

talking about? Why would Archie want to kill you?'

'He seems to think,' said the woman with the tattoo, 'that I murdered his father.'

The Head Teacher stared at her.

So did Archie.

'I saw him stealing a handbag,' said the woman with the tattoo, 'from someone he'd mugged in the car park, and I was coming down to tell the office to call the police, when I found him in the hallway and he gave me this note.' She held it out. 'Here. You can read it yourself.'

The Head Teacher took the note. '*You murdered my father . . .*' he said, reading it aloud, '*. . . and for this you must die.*' He looked at Archie, puzzled. 'You *really* think Miss Hurrell murdered your father?'

'Ho!' said Archie. 'Ha horse hot!'

'So why did you write this?' asked Mr Gunn. 'I don't understand how . . .' He stopped, and let out a sigh of relief. 'Ah, Cyd! Thank goodness you're here!'

Archie was as relieved as the Head Teacher to see Cyd. She was his best friend and, more importantly, Cyd was the one who seemed to sort everything out when odd things happened to him.

'Miss Hurrell says Archie mugged someone in the car park, stole their bag, then came into school and tried to murder her,' said Mr Gunn. 'You don't know what really happened, do you?'

'I've already told you what happened!' said the woman with the tattoo. 'He came at me with a knife—'

'Please!' The Head Teacher held up his hand and turned back to Cyd. 'Can you explain any of this?'

'Well, I can explain about the note,' said Cyd, who had been studying it. 'I think you were reading the wrong side. The *You murdered my father* bit is the first line of a story we have to write for Miss Jensen. On the other side it says *Mrs Boyd is in the car park with her arm stuck down a drain*. I expect that's what Archie was trying to tell you. He probably found her, and she asked him to go and get help.'

'Hess!' said Archie. 'Hat's hite!'

'I expect she asked him to take her bag to the kitchens as well,' Cyd continued, thoughtfully, 'so that they had the menu and could make a start on lunch.'

'And what about the knife?' asked the Head Teacher.

'Well,' said Cyd, 'I'm only guessing, but Archie may have wanted to show Miss Hurrell the menu, to explain why he had the bag, and had to take out the knife to get it.' She looked at Archie. 'Is that right?'

'Hess,' said Archie, looking very relieved. 'Hess! Hat's hite!'

There was a long pause.

'I . . . I don't believe it!' said Miss Hurrell.

'No,' said Mr Gunn. 'Nobody ever does.'

The Head Teacher sorted everything out very efficiently. He sent Archie and Cyd to the kitchens with Mrs Boyd's bag, he sent Miss Hurrell, the woman with the tattoo, back to her classroom, and then went out to the car park to look after Mrs Boyd.

On the way back from the kitchens, Cyd told Archie about their new teacher.

'She's quite interesting, really,' said Cyd. 'Mr Gunn told us she used to be a professional wrestler.'

'Hot hahenned,' said Archie, 'hoo Hiss Hensen?' He was trying to say *What happened to Miss Jensen*, their old teacher.

'She's in hospital,' Cyd explained. 'Miss

Hurrell's looking after our class until she comes back.'

'How hong hill hat he?' asked Archie.

'Mr Gunn said maybe a few days. Perhaps a week.'

'Ha heek?' Archie sighed. He liked Miss Jensen, because when odd things happened to him, she never got upset or angry, and she had *never* thrown him onto the ground and sat on him.

'Miss Hurrell's not that bad,' said Cyd, 'when you get to know her. I'm sure she didn't mean to hurt you.'

And indeed Miss Hurrell was most apologetic to Archie when he got back to the classroom.

'I'm *so* sorry,' she said. 'Mr Gunn told me about the odd things that happen to you, but when you gave me that message and then took a knife out of the bag I . . . I still can't believe it!' She lowered her voice. 'Is it true that something odd like that happens to you *every* day?'

'Hess,' said Archie.

'But why?'

'I hone ho,' said Archie.

'Archie's father has a theory,' said Cyd, 'that it's the Laws of Chance. He says that odd things happen to most people at some time in their lives, but not in an even number. Some people have a few odd things happen to them, some people don't have anything odd happen at all, and some people have odd things happen to them every day.'

'Like Archie?' said Miss Hurrell.

'Hess,' said Archie.

15

'The trick is not to get too upset about it,' said Cyd, 'and just keep smiling.'

And for the rest of the day that was what everyone tried to do.

Though Archie's mother was definitely not smiling when he got home and she saw the state of his clothes.

'That was a new shirt this morning,' she said, pointing to the torn collar. 'And now look! Anyone would think you'd been in a wrestling match!'

She went off to find a needle and thread.

'Honestly! I don't believe it, Archie!'

2. On Tuesday...

On Tuesday, when Archie and Cyd got to school, Mr Gunn told them that Miss Hurrell would not be coming back as their class teacher. After what happened on Monday, she had decided that life would be less stressful if she went back to being a professional wrestler.

'So you have another new teacher today,' said Mr Gunn. 'Her name is Miss Humber, and I've warned her about the odd things that happen to you.' He smiled encouragingly at Archie. 'I think you'll like her.'

Archie *did* like Miss Humber. She was a round, jolly woman, almost as wide as she was tall, and the first thing she did when she saw Archie was tell him that, if anything odd happened, he was not to worry, but to come straight to her.

In the morning, nothing odd did happen, but in the afternoon Miss Humber told her class she would show them how to make a fruit salad.

'A fresh fruit salad,' she said, 'is much better for you than cakes, and biscuits, and sweets, and ice cream, and doughnuts, and chocolate croissants and buns covered in thick white icing and . . .' She paused, and then added. 'A fruit salad keeps us all healthy and happy!'

Everyone in the class was given a different task. Some children had to peel the fruit and chop it up. Some were sent down to the kitchens to boil up the skins into a syrup, and some were given cameras to take pictures of the whole process so they could make a display afterwards.

Archie's job was peeling the bananas.

Miss Humber gave him a bag with the bananas in it, which he carried over to his table. He was about to reach inside, when he saw something moving.

It was a spider.

A big one.

'Miss Humber,' said Archie. 'There's a spider in here.'

On the other side of the room, Miss Humber was showing someone how to cut up a pineapple.

'Just pick it up and put it out the window,' she called back. 'There's no need to be frightened of spiders!'

'Oh,' said Archie, 'all right,' and he was reaching into the bag, when Cyd appeared beside him.

'I think you should leave it alone,' she said, 'until I've looked up what it is.'

Cyd went to the class laptop, tapped at the computer for a moment, then pointed to the screen.

'Hmmm,' she said. 'That's the one, isn't it?'

The picture she had found did indeed look exactly like the spider sitting on top of the bananas in Archie's bag. The writing beneath said that it was a Brazilian Wandering Spider.

'It's wandered quite a long way from

Brazil,' said Archie.

'It's sometimes known as the banana spider . . .' Cyd was reading the information from the screen, '. . . because that's where it likes to hide.'

'What are the red pouches on the front?' asked Archie.

'Those are the poison sacs,' said Cyd. 'It says here that it's the most venomous spider in the world.' She looked up. 'I think you'd better tell Miss Humber.'

Miss Humber took the news quite well, considering. She went a bit pale when Cyd

21

explained that the spider's bite could paralyse and even kill small children, but then she pulled back her shoulders, walked over to the bag and carefully peered inside.

'I can't see anything,' she said.

Archie looked as well, and found the spider had gone.

'Perhaps it's burrowed back down into the bananas,' he said.

'Or it could have climbed out while we were talking to you,' suggested Cyd.

'Well, we can't afford to take any risks,' said Miss Humber, and she strode to the front of the classroom. 'Listen carefully, everyone! It's possible we have a poisonous spider in the room and, as we don't know where it might be hiding—'

'It said on the computer . . .' interrupted Cyd '. . . that it likes to hide in places that are dark and warm. Like people's clothing.'

'Thank you,' said Miss Humber. 'Anyway, as I said, we don't know where it might be, so I want you all to put down whatever you're doing, and go downstairs to— What? What is it?'

There were twenty-three children in the classroom and they were all staring in silence at Miss Humber. Or, more precisely, at her trousers.

Miss Humber was wearing a pair of bright pink trousers and there was a bulge partway up one of the legs that seemed to be moving. Miss

Humber stared down as the bulge travelled further and further up. At first she seemed frozen to the spot, but when she did move, it was with an impressive speed.

She reached for the waistband of her trousers, and had pulled them down and thrown them to one side quicker than you could blink.

'Is it still on me?' she asked, peering down at her legs.

Reassuringly, the only thing to be seen on Miss Humber was a large pair of underpants, decorated with pictures of assorted sweets.

'It's all right,' said Cyd. 'It's over there.' She pointed to where Miss Humber's trousers had landed, just in front of the door. The spider was sitting on top of them.

'Keep back, everyone!' said Miss Humber. 'Keep well back!' And twenty-three children moved hurriedly to the opposite corner of the room.

'How are we going to get out, Miss?' asked

one boy, nervously. 'We're trapped, aren't we!'

And he was right. The only way out of the classroom was through the door and the spider was now sitting directly beneath the door handle. Someone would have to get very close to the spider to open the door, then push it to one side . . .

'We could shout for help,' suggested someone.

'It said on the computer,' said Cyd, 'that loud noises make a Brazilian Wandering Spider more aggressive.'

Someone else suggested they all climb out of the window and down a drainpipe, but Miss Humber thought that wasn't safe. They were still debating what to do when the door swung open, pushing the spider and the trousers towards the wall, and Mr Gunn came in.

'I thought I'd see how things were going,' he said, 'in case . . .' His voice trailed off. 'Miss Humber? You're not wearing any trousers!'

'No,' said Miss Humber. 'I'm afraid we have

a situation here, Mr Gunn. Archie has found a spider.'

The Head Teacher frowned. 'A spider?'

'A Brazilian Wandering Spider,' said Cyd, and she explained about it being poisonous, how its venom could paralyse and kill small children and how, if threatened, it could move faster than a leaping tiger.

'I see . . .' Mr Gunn took a deep breath. 'And where is this spider now?'

'It was in my trousers,' said Miss Humber. 'That's why I took them off.'

She pointed to where they lay on the floor

at the Head Teacher's feet. He looked down, and then moved hurriedly away.

'We need to get everyone out of here,' he said, 'and then somewhere safe. We'll start with you, I think, Archie. If you'd like to move towards the door . . .'

Now that the door was open, it should have been quite easy to leave, but Archie had only taken a few steps forward when he heard a gasp from twenty-three voices behind him, and then heard the Head Teacher's voice saying, 'Stay where you are, Archie! Don't move!'

'Why? What is it?' he asked, though a part of him already knew.

'It's on your back,' Cyd told him. 'I don't know how it got there, but it's crawling up your shirt.'

'Hang on!' said Mr Gunn, 'I'm going to try something . . .'

He picked up a bowl of chopped strawberries from the table beside him and threw the fruit at Archie's back. Unfortunately most of the fruit missed the spider, and the pieces that did hit it only succeeded in making it angry. It reared up on its back legs with a hissing sound.

Mr Gunn looked round the classroom. 'Anyone got any other ideas?'

'Yes,' said Miss Humber. 'I have.'

Because Archie was facing the other way, he didn't see what happened next, but Cyd told him afterwards that it was one of the most amazing things she had ever witnessed. The spider was still climbing up Archie's back and was almost on his neck when Miss Humber stepped forward, reached out her hand, and grabbed it. With the legs waving and wriggling through her fingers, she calmly carried it over to an empty saucepan, dropped it inside, and put the lid on.

'Oh, bravo, Miss Humber, bravo!' said Mr Gunn as he crossed the classroom to join her. 'But . . . are you all right?'

'I think so.' Miss Humber opened the hand that had grabbed the spider and stared down at it. There were two small punctures at the base of her thumb. 'I don't think it had time to inject much poison before . . . before . . .'

She was swaying slightly on her feet and then her eyes closed and she crashed to the floor.

'The good news,' said Mr Gunn, an hour later when he returned to the classroom, 'is that the men from the council have taken away the spider, and that Miss Humber is going to be fine. They've given her injections to help with the pain and they say, in a day or two, she'll be able to move her arms and legs again quite normally.'

He smiled as he looked around the class. 'I think we all know what a brave thing it was that she did, and the last thing she told me in the ambulance, before her jaw became paralysed, was that she hoped you would all finish off the fruit salad you were making. She wanted me to remind you that a fruit salad keeps us all healthy and happy!'

So the class finished making the fruit salad, and perhaps the only person who was *not* happy at the end of the day was Archie's mother, who couldn't understand why there were strawberry stains all down the back of his shirt.

'What on earth do you *do* in that school?' she demanded, as she carried his shirt off to the kitchen to put it in the wash.

'Honestly! I don't believe it, Archie!'

3. On Wednesday . . .

On Wednesday, Archie's class had another new teacher. This one was called Miss Henley, and she was young and very beautiful.

But although she was young and beautiful, you could tell Miss Henley was not a *happy* person. There was a deep sadness in her eyes that came out in the way she spoke, and in the way she taught her class.

In art, for instance, she asked them to draw a picture of what it might be like to be the only person left alive after a nuclear war. In maths, she set them problems like, 'If there are fifty people in your street and ninety percent of them die of bird-flu, how many will be left?' And for their literacy homework, Miss Henley said she wanted everyone to write about how it felt to lose someone they loved.

'Maybe you've had a pet that died,' she said, 'or a grandparent who passed away, or a best friend who moved to another country so that you never saw them again . . .' She paused to lend a hankie to two girls who were already crying. 'We've all had experiences like this,' she continued. 'I myself once lost someone I loved very much and . . . I want you to describe how unhappy that sort of thing can make you feel.'

Archie was not looking forward to this homework. It was all right for Cyd – she could write about her father who was away in the army and whom she hadn't seen for months – but he couldn't think of anything to write about himself.

'I can't remember losing anyone,' he said, as he and Cyd collected their coats and bags at the end of school.

'Seriously?' Cyd was understandably surprised. 'I'd have thought, with all the odd things happening to you, that you lost someone almost every week.'

'No one I really cared about,' said Archie. His face furrowed in thought. 'I had a pet ant once that—'

But he never got to say what happened to the ant, because at that moment Cyd discovered she'd forgotten her reading book and they had to go back up to the classroom to get it.

The classroom was empty when they got there but, as Cyd collected her book, they heard a strange noise coming from the stockroom cupboard. When they went to see what it was, they found Miss Henley inside, sitting on a pile of dictionaries, gazing at a photograph and crying quietly.

'Miss Henley?' said Archie. 'Are you OK?'

'Oh yes! Yes, I'm fine!' Miss Henley blew her nose on a tissue and smiled at him through her tears. 'Don't mind me, I'm just . . .' She put the photo back in her bag. 'Is there something you need?'

'I forgot my reading book,' said Cyd. 'Are you *sure* you're OK?'

Miss Henley repeated that she was, and the two children turned to leave. Unfortunately the stockroom door had swung shut behind them when they went in and when Archie tried to open it, the handle came off in his hand.

'I suppose this is one of the "odd" things that are always happening to you,' said Miss Henley. 'Mr Gunn warned me about that this morning. Well, let's see what we can do!'

There are several ways you can try to get out of a small room when the handle has come off the door and in the next half-hour, Archie, Cyd and Miss Henley tried all of them. They tried fitting the handle back on the door. They tried shouting and screaming for help. Miss Henley even tried bashing the door down with a fire extinguisher, but nothing worked.

'I'm afraid we'll just have to wait,' she said, sitting back down on her pile of dictionaries. 'Someone will come and rescue us eventually.'

'You think so?' asked Archie.

'I'm sure of it!' said Miss Henley, confidently. 'Tomorrow morning, when the other children get here—'

'Tomorrow morning!' interrupted Cyd. 'You mean we could be stuck here all night?'

'It's not that bad,' said Miss Henley. 'We'll manage.' She gestured to the shelves around her. 'At least we've got plenty to read, so we can—'

There was a *plink* sound and the bulb in the ceiling went out, plunging the room into darkness.

'Don't panic!' said Miss Henley. 'I've got a box of matches in my bag!'

A moment later there was a scratching

sound and Miss Henley's face appeared above a small yellow flame.

'Now,' she said, 'I seem to remember seeing some candles in here . . .'

Archie climbed up onto a shelf to get down the box of candles, which were left over from a project Miss Jensen had been doing on steam power. Just as he reached them, however, the match Miss Henley was holding burned down to the point where it was singeing her fingers and she dropped it.

It fell, still alight, into her handbag which, as well as being full of paper tissues, contained a leaking bottle of nail varnish.

Nail varnish, in case you didn't know, is highly inflammable.

There was a *whoompf* noise as Miss Henley's bag burst into flames, and a brief moment of panic while Miss Henley tried to stamp out the fire with her feet and Archie tried to beat it out with his coat, before Cyd picked up the fire extinguisher and sprayed the bag with foam.

Some minutes later, by the light of a candle, they were able to review the situation. There were black marks on the wall, Archie's coat was badly scorched, and there was a puddle of foam on the floor, but the only real damage seemed to be to Miss Henley's bag, most of which had been burned away.

'Phew!' said Archie. 'That was a close one!'

Miss Henley did not answer. Instead, she reached into the sodden remains of her bag and took out the burned corner that was all that was left of a photograph. She began

crying again, and it was almost a minute before she had recovered enough to wipe the tears from her face with a piece of kitchen towel Cyd found for her.

'I'm sorry,' said the teacher. 'But it was the only photo I had of him, you see.'

'Only photo of who?' asked Cyd.

'My fiancé.' Miss Henley let out a long sigh. 'Gary. We met on holiday eight months ago, fell in love, and we were going to get married as soon as we got back to England. But I had to fly back the day before him, so I gave him my address and phone number. He said he would call me as soon as he was home and' – Miss Henley gave a little sob – 'he never did.'

'Why not?' asked Cyd.

'I don't know!' Miss Henley lifted her arms in despair. 'Perhaps he didn't really love me. Perhaps he forgot. Perhaps . . . perhaps he's dead!'

The tears were running down her face again.

'Maybe,' said Cyd thoughtfully, 'we could send a message.'

'But I don't know where he lives!' said Miss Henley.

'She can't send him a message if she doesn't know where he lives,' said Archie.

'I was thinking of a message asking someone to come and rescue us,' said Cyd. She pointed to an air vent in the wall up near the ceiling. 'If we take the cover off that vent, write a message on a piece of paper, fold it up as a paper dart and throw it through the hole in the wall, whoever finds it can come and rescue us!'

'You think someone would find it?' said Miss Henley, doubtfully.

'They might not find *one* message,' said Cyd, 'but look at all the paper we've got!' She gestured to the piles of paper stacked on the shelves around the stockroom. 'We can send out hundreds. Someone's bound to notice eventually.'

'That is brilliant!' said Archie. 'Come on then, let's do it!'

Miss Henley wrote out the message in big letters on a piece of paper. It said:

> We are stuck in the stockroom on the first floor of Tetley Junior School. Please tell the Head Teacher or the police and come and rescue us.

Cyd folded it up as a paper dart and passed it to Archie who had successfully taken off the cover of the air vent, revealing a round hole. He took the dart and launched it into the world.

Miss Henley had already written the same message on another piece of paper when, even before Cyd had finished folding it and Archie could throw it out, they heard footsteps running down the corridor and into the classroom. A moment later the door had opened and two men were standing in the doorway gazing at them. One of them was Mr Gunn, the Head Teacher.

'I don't believe it!' he said, staring at the foam on the floor, the broken vent and the burned handbag. 'What happened?'

45

'The door handle came off,' Archie explained, 'and we were trapped.'

'I'm glad you found the note,' said Cyd, pointing to the piece of paper the Head Teacher was holding. 'We thought we might have to stay here all night.'

'Well, *I* didn't find it,' said Mr Gunn. 'He did.' He pointed to the young man standing beside him, wearing a postman's uniform. 'He was walking down the road just outside the school when your dart landed at his feet. He brought it in to me and . . .' He paused, looking anxiously at Miss Henley. 'Are you all right?'

Miss Henley did not answer, and Archie could see why the Head Teacher was concerned. She had not moved or spoken since the door to the stockroom had opened. All she had done was stare, open-mouthed, at the man in the postman's uniform.

'Gary?' she said, her voice no more than a whisper. 'Is that you?'

'Penny!' The young man knelt down and took Miss Henley's hands in his own. 'I don't believe it! Penny! Have I really found you at last?'

'You . . . you've been looking for me?' asked Miss Henley.

'I have done nothing but search for you for the last eight months!' said the man, and in a great sweeping motion he took Miss Henley into his arms and kissed her.

'Please!' said Mr Gunn. 'Please! Not in front of the children!'

An hour later, as they were walking home, Archie and Cyd could still hardly believe what had happened. They had listened, entranced, to Gary's story of how, eight months before, on the day he was meant to fly back to England, he had been injured while trying to rescue a kitten from the hotel balcony.

'I was in hospital for three days,' he said, sitting in Mr Gunn's office with Miss Henley beside him. 'But when they gave me my clothes back, the address and phone number you had given me was gone, and the only part of it I could remember was the name of the town. So I moved here, got a job as a postman and hoped that one day I'd see you in the street, or find your name on a letter.' He held Miss Henley's hands tightly in his own as he spoke. 'And now I've found you again, I shall never let you go!'

'It's like something you read about in story books, isn't it?' said Cyd, as they walked up the road to her house. 'The two of them are going

to live happily ever after, and it's all thanks to you, Archie! I think you should feel really pleased!'

And Archie did feel quite pleased – at least he did until he got home and his mother saw him.

'What have you done to your coat?' she demanded, pointing to the scorch marks caused by the fire in the stockroom. 'And what are all those stains round the bottom of your trousers?'

'Honestly!' She shook her head. 'I don't believe it, Archie!'

4. On Thursday . . .

On Thursday, Archie's class had yet another new teacher.

Mrs Hemp was an elderly woman with grey hair and a hearing aid, who had in fact retired three years before, but still occasionally taught in schools when she was needed.

Mr Gunn did his best to warn to her about Archie.

'We're not sure *why* something odd happens to him every day,' he said, 'but you will need to watch out for it.'

Mrs Hemp, however, only laughed. 'I've been teaching for forty years,' she said, 'and I've seen children do just about everything. Nothing odd is going to surprise me, I promise you!'

Mr Gunn hoped that she was right, but
what happened later that day came as a
surprise to both of them.

It was about halfway through the afternoon
when Mrs Hemp appeared in the Head
Teacher's office, carrying a school bag. She
was accompanied by a small black and white
dog.

'You'll never believe what's happened!' she
said.

'If this is about Archie, then I probably
won't,' said Mr Gunn. 'What's he done this
time?'

Mrs Hemp pointed dramatically to the
terrier at her feet. 'He's turned into a dog,'
she said.

'You're right,' said Mr Gunn. 'I don't
believe it.'

'I didn't either at first,' said Mrs Hemp, 'but
it's the only explanation.' She sat herself in a
chair opposite the Head Teacher and gestured

to the dog to sit beside her. 'If you want, you
can ask him yourself.'

'Ask him?' said Mr Gunn.

'I know he can't speak English,' said Mrs
Hemp, 'not while he's a dog, but I've given
him a sort of code to use. One *woof* means
"yes", and two means "no". Go on! Ask him if
he's Archie Coates!'

Mr Gunn looked at the dog, who was
sitting obediently on the floor. 'Are you Archie
Coates?' he asked.

'*Woof!*' said the dog.

'Really?'

'*Woof!*'

'You're not just . . . making it up?'

'*Woof, woof!*' said the dog.

The Head Teacher leaned back in his chair and frowned. 'A lot of dogs bark when you talk to them,' he said. 'It's a coincidence.'

'No, it's not,' said Mrs Hemp, firmly. 'I've been asking him questions for the last ten minutes and he's answered every one of them correctly! The poor boy has turned into a dog. And it's not the first time this has happened to him!'

Mr Gunn took off his glasses and pinched the bridge of his nose. 'What makes you think that?'

'I heard him telling Cyd about it in the playground this morning,' said Mrs Hemp. 'I heard him describe, in some detail, how he turned into a dog last night, how his parents threw him out of the house and how he had to search for food . . .'

'Children have very vivid imaginations,' said Mr Gunn.

'I agree,' said Mrs Hemp, 'and I presumed that's all it was. Until lunchtime.' She leaned forward and continued in a low, confidential tone. 'That was when I saw this dog trotting down the corridor towards my classroom. I followed it, went inside and do you know what I saw?'

'A dog?' suggested Mr Gunn.

'Archie!' said Mrs Hemp. 'No sign of the dog. Just Archie Coates. And when he'd gone I searched the entire classroom. But there was no dog! I saw a dog go in, but only a boy went out.'

'That is certainly odd,' Mr Gunn agreed,

'but as I told you this morning—'

'And this afternoon,' continued Mrs Hemp, ignoring the interruption, 'I saw Archie going into the men's cloakroom on the ground floor.'

'What was he doing in there?' asked Mr Gunn. The cloakroom on the ground floor was only supposed to be used by teachers.

'That's what I wanted to know,' said Mrs Hemp. 'So I waited outside for a while, but then I heard noises – animal noises – and when I went inside . . .'

'Yes?'

'When I went inside I found this dog' – Mrs Hemp pointed dramatically to the animal at her feet – 'sitting on a pile of school clothes, and no sign of Archie! There is only one possible explanation. The boy turned into a dog and his clothes fell off around him.' She looked down at the terrier. 'That is what happened, isn't it?'

'*Woof!*' said the dog.

Mr Gunn opened his mouth to speak,

closed it again, then consulted a timetable on his desk.

'According to this,' he said, 'Archie is doing Sports at the moment with Miss Roberts, out on the field. Perhaps the first thing to do is find out if—'

There was a knock at the door, and Cyd appeared.

'Miss Roberts sent me to tell you,' she said, 'that Archie's supposed to be doing Sports out on the field, but he hasn't turned up.'

'There you are!' Mrs Hemp turned in her chair to face Cyd. 'Don't worry, dear! He's safe here with us.'

'Is he?' Cyd looked quickly round the Head Teacher's office. 'Where?'

'Here,' Mrs Hemp pointed to the terrier beside her. 'I'm afraid he's turned into a dog again.'

'*Woof!*' said the dog.

Cyd stared at Mrs Hemp, and then at the dog. She knew that teachers could get strange ideas sometimes, but this one was . . .

'That's not Archie,' she said. 'It's a dog. He's called Ruffles!'

Mrs Hemp frowned, and turned to the dog. 'Is your name Ruffles?'

'*Woof woof!*' said the dog.

'Who's Ruffles?' asked Mr Gunn.

'Ruffles belongs to Laura Wilde,' said Cyd. 'She's only had him a couple of weeks and he's supposed to be at home, but sometimes he escapes and comes to school to see her. Then we all have to hide him because we don't want Laura to get into trouble.'

'I'm sorry,' said Mrs Hemp, 'but this animal has told me quite definitely that he is Archie Coates.' She looked at the dog. 'Isn't that right?'

'*Woof!*' said the dog.

'Mrs Hemp thinks that he's speaking in code,' Mr Gunn explained. 'One *woof* for "yes", and two for "no".'

'He's not speaking in code!' said Cyd. 'He's barking!'

And he wasn't the only one, she thought.

'So why did Mrs Hemp overhear Archie telling you this morning about turning into a dog last night?' asked Mr Gunn.

'What?' Cyd looked puzzled for a moment,

but then her face cleared. 'Oh, you mean the dream!'

'Dream?'

'Yes,' said Cyd. 'Archie was telling me in break this morning he had a dream last night where he turned into a dog, went down to the chip shop and then shrank to the size of a pea and vanished through a hole in the floor. It wasn't real,' she added, in case there was any doubt.

Mrs Hemp looked rather confused.

'But I *saw* him change,' she said. 'At lunchtime. I saw a dog go into a classroom and then, when I went in, there was no dog, just Archie.'

'If Archie found the dog in school, he would have hidden him,' said Cyd. 'Like I told you, we don't want Laura to get into trouble. Was he carrying a bag?'

'He had his school bag, yes, but . . .'

'He'll have put the dog in the bag,' said Cyd, confidently, 'and then taken it to the men's cloakroom on the ground floor. It's safe to leave him there, you see, because no one uses it. Then he'll tell Laura to collect him at the end of the day.'

'But . . . but . . . I followed Archie into the cloakroom this afternoon!' Mrs Hemp was visibly confused. 'And he wasn't there! There was just a pile of clothes on the floor and the dog in the middle of it. How do you explain that?'

'I can't,' said Cyd. 'But I expect Archie can.'

'Which brings us back to the real problem,' said Mr Gunn. 'Where exactly is Archie?' He looked hopefully at Cyd.

'Well, I don't *know*,' said Cyd, 'but if he was last seen going into the staff cloakroom, and then someone else went in and took away his bag and all his clothes, I should imagine he's probably still there.'

The Head Teacher stood up. 'Let's go and find out, shall we?'

The three of them strode out of the Head's office and along the corridor to the cloakroom. The dog followed them.

When Mr Gunn pushed open the door, the cloakroom seemed to be empty.

'Archie?' said Cyd. 'Are you in here?'

'Thank goodness!' said a voice. 'I've been stuck in here for—'

Archie's head appeared round the side of the shower stall, but he stopped in mid-sentence when he saw the Head and Mrs Hemp.

'Someone's taken all my clothes,' he said.
'Does anyone know where they are?'

'*Woof!*' said the dog.

'It was a nightmare,' Archie told Cyd as the
two of them walked home. 'I'm telling you, the
whole thing was a complete nightmare.'

'I still don't understand,' said Cyd. 'What happened after you found Ruffles and put him in the men's cloakroom? I mean, why did you go back later? And why did you take all your clothes off?'

'I went back to check he was OK,' Archie explained. 'You know how he can start howling if he's left on his own for too long. So I thought I'd call in before getting changed for Sports and give him a biscuit. Then, when I got to the cloakroom, he was really pleased

to see me. He jumped on my lap and he had his paws on my shoulders, and he was licking my face. He was very excited . . . like, very excited . . .'

'Oh, no!' said Cyd. 'He didn't!'

'He did,' said

Archie. 'He weed all down the front of my shirt and down my trousers. I was soaking . . .'

'And that's why you took everything off?'

'Well, I couldn't go anywhere like that, could I?' said Archie. 'So I thought I'd get changed into my games kit. And then I thought, as there was a shower in there, it might be a good idea to have a wash first . . .'

'And when you got out of the shower, all your clothes had gone,' Cyd finished, sympathetically.

'My clothes, my bag with the games kit, the dog, everything!' Archie shook his head.

'I couldn't believe it! I had nothing to wear. There weren't even any paper towels!'

'Mrs Hemp did say how sorry she was,' said Cyd.

'I know,' Archie agreed, 'but it was still a nightmare. The whole thing.' He walked a few paces in silence before adding, 'Did you know Mr Gunn laughed when I told him? He thought it was funny! I mean . . . what is funny about being stuck in a room with no clothes, wondering if you'll have to walk through the school, naked, to tell someone what happened?'

'Well,' said Cyd, 'it is a *bit* funny. If you think about it.'

Archie thought about it and, slowly, a smile replaced the frown on his face.

'I suppose it is a bit,' he said. He turned to his friend. 'Mrs Hemp didn't *really* think I'd turned into a dog, did she?'

'She was *positive* you had,' said Cyd. 'And I think she almost convinced Mr Gunn.'

They both laughed.

Archie's mother, however, was definitely not laughing when she saw him. She wanted to know why he had come home in his games kit, and what had happened to his school clothes.

'And what's this stain down the front of your shirt?' she demanded, as she took it out of his bag. 'It's all down your trousers as well,

and what . . . what's that smell?' Her nose
wrinkled in disgust. 'Is that what I think it is?'
She held the clothes at arm's length.
'Honestly! I don't believe it, Archie!'

5. On Friday . . .

On Friday, when Archie arrived at school, the Head Teacher called him into his office.

'I wonder,' he said, closing the door behind them, 'if you'd mind not going into class today?'

'You want me to miss all my lessons?' asked Archie.

'Yes.' Mr Gunn sat down behind his desk. 'You see, Mrs Hemp will not be coming back after what happened yesterday, which means we have lost four teachers so far this week and, although I've managed to get another replacement, this is the last one. They don't have any more.'

'Oh,' said Archie.

'We'll be all right when Miss Jensen gets back,' said the Head. 'She knows how to cope with all the odd things that happen to you but, until then, I'd like you to stay in here with me.' He pointed to a chair and table in the corner. 'I've set up somewhere for you to work.'

Archie didn't really like the idea of being on his own all day, but it was not quite as bad as he had expected. He had often wondered what Head Teachers *did* during the day and now, sitting in the corner of Mr Gunn's office, he was able to find out.

The Head Teacher seemed to spend most of his time sorting out problems for people who came to see him. He sorted out the plumber who wanted to know if he could fit a new toilet in the girls' lavatory. He sorted out the builders who wanted to know where they could put their skip. And he sorted out teachers like Miss Roberts, who wanted to know how to make hydrogen gas for a science experiment. And through it all, Archie was able to watch and listen.

At least he was until the middle of the morning, when Mr Gunn looked at his diary and told Archie he would have to leave him on his own for the next hour or two.

'We've got a visit from the Health and Safety Inspector,' he said, and a slightly worried look crossed his face. 'He's a new man – I've not met him before – but I'll have to show him round the school. It's important that he gives us a good report.'

The Inspector's name was Mr Halibut, and

his visit did not get off to a good start.

'I must warn you,' he said, when the secretary showed him into Mr Gunn's office, 'that I am not impressed by what I've seen so far.'

'But you haven't seen anything yet,' protested Mr Gunn. 'All you've done is walk in from the car park!'

'And in that short walk,' said Mr Halibut, severely, 'I saw children playing outside, in the sunshine, without sunhats. I saw the outside door to a classroom left open, so that any passing axe murderer could walk straight in.'

He sniffed. 'And coming into this office I see that you openly encourage the consumption of sugary sweets.' He pointed to a glass bowl of lollipops on Mr Gunn's desk.

The Head Teacher stared at him. 'What happened to Mr Stevens?' he asked. 'He's the one who normally does our Health and Safety inspection.'

'Mr Stevens is busy,' said Mr Halibut, stiffly. 'If you would be so good as to show me round the school?'

Mr Gunn did not answer immediately. For several seconds he drummed his fingers on the desk before saying, 'I'm sorry, I can't show you round myself. I have another appointment. But Archie here can take you.'

Archie blinked. The Head Teacher was usually very careful not to let him get too close to visitors, in case something 'odd' happened.

'Mr Gunn,' he said, 'are you sure that—'

'Quite sure, thank you!' Mr Gunn interrupted. 'I'd like you to take Mr Halibut round the school. Show him everything. Take as long as you need, all right?'

'All right,' said Archie.

He began his tour by taking Mr Halibut outside and showing him the Thinking Garden. It was a little fenced area where children could go when they wanted somewhere to sit quietly and think.

'What is that?' demanded Mr Halibut, pointing to a large stone with a hollow in it, containing the remains of two candles.

Archie explained that, if there was someone you cared about who might be in trouble, you could light a candle for them in the garden.

'My friend Cyd lights a candle here sometimes for her dad,' he said. 'He's in the army, and she hasn't seen him for—'

'I don't believe it!' said Mr Halibut. 'You mean your Head Teacher actually *hands out* matches and candles to his students?'

'Well, yes,' said Archie. 'Is that bad?'

'Of course it's bad!' said Mr Halibut. He

gestured round the Thinking Garden. 'This place is an Accident Waiting to Happen!'

In the next half hour, the Inspector saw a lot of things that he thought were Accidents Waiting to Happen. He was horrified to hear

that children were allowed to play under the trees at the edge of the field – where branches might fall off at any moment and kill them. He was appalled to discover that the school kept two goats. There are, he told Archie, at least nineteen diseases you can catch from goats, three of which are fatal. And he was deeply shocked when, on the path that led round the back of the school, Archie picked up a toy gun.

'I think it's Harry's,' said Archie. 'We had to come to school dressed as characters from a book last week, and he came as James Bond.'

'I don't believe it!' said Mr Halibut. 'Doesn't your Head Teacher know that playing with toy guns encourages violence? And from what I've heard, you have quite enough violence in this school already.'

'Do we?' said Archie.

Mr Halibut lowered his voice before replying. 'I heard a story,' he said, 'that earlier this week, a boy at this school threatened his teacher with a knife!'

'Oh, *that!*' said Archie. 'No, that was just a misunderstanding! I wasn't really threatening her.'

Mr Halibut stopped in his tracks.

'You . . . You were the one with the knife?'

'The trouble was,' said Archie, 'that Miss Hurrell thought that *I* thought that she'd murdered my father. I didn't, of course, it was just a misunderstanding, but then she saw me with the knife, and after she'd seen me with the other body in the car park . . .'

Archie stopped, because he could see that

Mr Halibut was not listening. He was backing away. Backing away quite fast and, Archie noticed, not looking where he was going. Behind him was a row of cones and a warning sign saying: BUILDERS AT WORK. KEEP AWAY! Mr Halibut, however, did not see it.

Archie tried to warn him. 'Stop, Mr Halibut!' he said. 'Please! Stop now!'

But Mr Halibut did not stop. Looking thoroughly frightened, he backed through the barrier of cones and continued moving backwards until he was up against the side of a skip.

'You need to come away from there, Mr Halibut!' Archie called. 'You need to come back towards me.'

He had quite forgotten, as he later told Cyd, that he was still holding the toy gun as he said this, and it was unfortunate that, at just that moment, Miss Roberts, in the classroom behind him, was doing her demonstration of how hydrogen gas, when ignited, makes a very loud *bang*. It was even more unfortunate that, at exactly the same time, one of the builders tossed a bit of concrete into the skip, which bounced up and grazed the side of Mr Halibut's head.

To understand why all these things together led to the accident that followed, you have to imagine how they looked from Mr Halibut's point of view.

Horrified at discovering that the boy who was taking him round the school was the same child who had, apparently, threatened a teacher with a knife earlier in the week, he now found this same boy was pointing a gun at him. He had thought the gun was a toy but, as Mr Halibut stood with his back to the skip, there was a loud bang and something hit the side of his head.

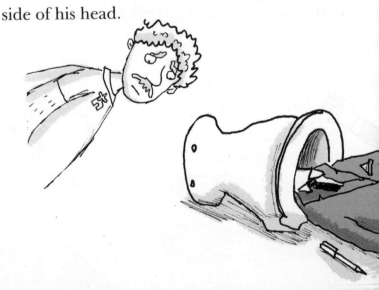

Putting his hand up to his temple, he found blood on his fingers and, perhaps understandably, came to the conclusion that he had been shot.

Before Archie could shoot him again he turned and, in blind panic, raced into the car park where Mr James, the plumber, was carrying in the new toilet for the girls' lavatory. Head down and sprinting for dear life, Mr Halibut ran straight into it with enough force to jam his head halfway down the bowl.

He sank to the ground, still with the toilet bowl on his head, and lay there, not moving.

'They've taken him off in the ambulance,' said Mr Gunn, when he got back to his office. 'There was quite a crowd in the end, watching.'

'Did they get the toilet bowl off his head?' asked Archie.

'They're going to do that at the hospital,' said the Head, 'but you needn't worry. I'm sure he's going to be fine, even if he did lose quite a lot of blood.' He looked at Archie. 'Are you all right yourself?'

Some of the blood Mr Halibut had lost had wound up down the front of Archie's shirt. The cut on the Inspector's head had been bleeding heavily when Archie ran over to try and help.

'I'm OK,' said Archie, 'but . . . but I'm really sorry.'

'Nothing for you to be sorry about,' said Mr

Gunn. 'None of it was your fault, was it?'

'But Mr Halibut's going to be so angry, isn't he?' said Archie. 'Which means he'll give the school a really bad report and—'

'As it happens, Mr Halibut won't be giving any reports in the near future,' said Mr Gunn. 'He'll be in hospital for some time, so I've arranged for our inspection to be done by Mr Stevens. He's a good man. Very sensible.'

Archie was relieved to hear it, but he still felt bad about Mr Halibut. 'I can't help thinking,' he said, 'that if I hadn't been there, probably nothing would have happened.'

'Maybe not,' said Mr Gunn, 'but I don't think we should worry too much about it.'

Certainly, Mr Gunn did not seem to be too worried. He sat at his desk, leaned back in his chair and there was even the trace of a smile on his face as gazed out of the window.

'Here,' he said, and he spun round and pointed to the glass bowl of sweets on his desk. 'Have a lolly.'

And then, to Archie's astonishment, he added. 'In fact . . . have two!'

'I don't believe it!' said Cyd, as she and Archie walked home at the end of the day. 'He gave you *two* lollies?'

You had to have done something very special to be given a lolly from the bowl on Mr Gunn's desk. It was a bit like a soldier being awarded the Victoria Cross, and nobody had ever been told to take two.

'I thought he was going to be really cross with me,' said Archie, passing one of the lollies to his friend, 'but he wasn't. He told me not to worry about it.'

'We missed everything, up in the

classroom,' said Cyd, sadly. 'We didn't see the accident. We didn't even see the ambulance.' She sighed. 'A man with a toilet on his head running round the car park, and we missed it all.'

'You might get to see it on Monday,' Archie told her. 'Mrs Clay filmed the whole thing from her classroom, and Mr Gunn said he was going to show it in assembly.'

'Really?' Cyd's face brightened, and maybe it was the thought of the film, or maybe it was the lolly from Mr Gunn's sweet jar, but she seemed to be in a much better mood after that.

Archie's mother, however, was definitely *not* in a good mood when she saw the splashes of blood down the front of his shirt.

'Is it really too much to ask,' she said, 'that you come home one day – *one day* – without your clothes needing to be boiled clean?'

'Honestly,' she muttered, as she sent him upstairs to get changed. 'I don't believe it, Archie!'

6. On Saturday . . .

On Saturday, Cyd suggested that she and Archie visit Miss Jensen, their class teacher, in hospital.

'I think she needs to know,' said Cyd, 'how important it is that she comes back to school as soon as possible.'

'*Is* it important?' asked Archie.

'Of course it is!' said Cyd. 'You don't want to be stuck in Mr Gunn's office all next week, do you? I'll ask Mum to take us. You go and pick some flowers.'

Cyd's mother was a nurse, and she drove them to the hospital and told them how to get to Miss Jensen's ward. They found their teacher sitting in a chair by her bed, looking very well.

'I *am* very well,' she said, when Archie asked. 'I've never felt better.'

'Does that mean you'll be back in school on Monday?' asked Cyd, eagerly.

'Unfortunately not,' said Miss Jensen. 'They're waiting for the results of some tests they've done. Then someone has to decide what medicine I need. I could be here for days yet.' She looked at the flowers the children had brought. 'These are lovely. Could one of you get some water for them?'

Archie said he would and, leaving Cyd with Miss Jensen, he went out into the corridor to find somewhere he could fill the jam jar he had brought, with water.

The accident happened on his way back.

Walking down the corridor, some of the water splashed out of the jar and, rather than leave a wet patch on the floor that someone might slip on, Archie bent down to mop it up with his sleeve.

The porter, coming out of the lift with a hospital trolley, didn't see him until it was too late. He pushed his trolley out into the corridor and the end of it banged straight into Archie's head.

Archie gave a little cry and sprawled on the floor, his jam jar of water rolling away beside him.

The porter came running round and knelt down beside Archie. 'I'm sorry, I never saw you! Are you all right?'

Archie sat up, slowly. 'My head hurts,' he said.

'I'm not surprised.' The porter peered at the back of Archie's head. 'You took quite a knock. We'd better get someone to look at that.'

He sat Archie on his trolley and wheeled him off down the corridor. 'I've got a friend in the children's ward,' he said. 'She'll look after you!'

The porter's friend was a nurse with short, dark hair and a friendly smile. She took Archie into a room with a bed and an armchair and examined the lump on the back of his head.

'He gave you quite a thump, didn't he?' she said cheerfully. 'Wait here. I'll get you a glass of water and an aspirin.'

Archie sat in the armchair and waited.

'How's the head?' asked a voice, and he looked up to see another nurse, this one tall and wearing glasses, looking down at him.

'Well, it still hurts a bit,' Archie told her.

'This should help,' said the nurse, holding out a little plastic cup of medicine. 'You get that down you.'

Archie did as he was told and drank the medicine, which tasted rather nice.

'Now,' said the nurse. 'You know what's going to happen next?'

Archie shook his head.

'Well, it's nothing to worry about. We've got one of the doctors coming down shortly, and he'll explain it to you.'

The nurse with short, dark hair appeared in the doorway with a glass of water and an aspirin, but the tall nurse waved her away.

'It's all right,' she said. 'I'm looking after Archie!'

'Oh. OK!' The dark-haired nurse smiled at Archie and left.

'As I was saying,' said the tall nurse, 'the doctor will explain about the operation, so if there's anything you want to know, you ask him.'

The operation?

Archie hadn't thought the bang on his head had been *that* serious but, curiously, he wasn't really worried. There was a wonderfully relaxed and floaty feeling running through the muscles of his arms and legs and for some reason it was impossible to worry about anything.

'How's the head now?' asked the nurse.

'Issfine,' said Archie. And it was true. His head did not hurt any more and he was feeling calm, relaxed and without a care in the world.

'I told you the medicine would help,' said the nurse. 'Now, let's get you undressed and into bed!'

Cyd, meanwhile, had been telling Miss Jensen about all the things that had happened earlier in the week. She told her about Miss Hurrell, the teacher who thought Archie wanted to murder her, and about Miss Humber and the Brazilian Wandering Spider, and about Miss Henley getting trapped in the stockroom. She told her about Mrs Hemp thinking that Archie had turned into a dog, and then about the man from Health and Safety getting a toilet stuck on his head.

'Though I didn't actually see any of that

one,' Cyd admitted. 'Archie was taken out of the class, so I missed it.'

Miss Jensen gave a little sigh. 'I know how you feel,' she said. 'I've missed a whole week of Archie's adventures, stuck in here. And it looks as if I might have to miss another.' She paused for a moment. 'I wanted to ask if there was any news of your father coming home, but before I do . . . Archie's taking rather a long time getting that jar of water, isn't he? Do you think something's happened?'

'Hmm . . .' said Cyd. 'I'd better go and check.'

'Well, now!' The doctor stood at the foot of the bed and smiled down at Archie, who was dressed in a pair of hospital pyjamas. 'I'm the doctor who's going to put you to sleep for your operation and I came to see if you had any questions.'

Archie had to think quite hard before he remembered that he did have one question.

'This operation,' he said. 'What's it for?'

'Ah,' said the doctor. 'Well, the X-rays have shown us that there's a blood clot in your skull – that's what's been causing all the pain you've been getting – and what we're going to do is—'

'I don't believe it!' said a voice.

'Hi, Cyd!' Archie gave his friend a little wave.

'What are you doing in bed?' demanded Cyd.

'I'm going to have an operation!' said Archie. 'On my head!

Cyd stared coldly at the doctor. 'What've you done to him?' she demanded.

'We haven't done anything yet,' said the doctor, 'but, as I was just explaining, the pains Archie's been getting are caused by a blood clot in his skull. So we're going to put him to sleep, drill a little hole in the back of his head and—'

'No,' said Cyd, firmly. 'No, you're not.'

'It's all right.' The tall nurse put a hand on Cyd's shoulder. 'He won't feel a thing, I promise.'

'He won't feel anything,' said Cyd, 'because

you're not going to operate on him. There's obviously been a mistake.'

'We don't make mistakes at St James's,' said the doctor, stiffly. 'Your friend was brought in last night and—'

'My friend was not brought in last night,' said Cyd. 'He came in this morning with me to visit our teacher, and until half an hour ago he was absolutely fine. I don't know how he got into this bed, or why you want to drill a hole in his head, but you're not going to.'

'I'll call security,' said the nurse.

'How about you wait,' said Cyd, 'until you've checked if what I said is true. It won't be very difficult. You can ask our teacher, who's in the ward down the corridor. You can phone Archie's parents – I've got his number here – or you can talk to my mother, who's down in the nurse's restroom. You can do any of those things but there is no way I'm letting you do an operation on my friend Archie Coates.'

There was a moment's silence as the doctor looked at his clipboard, and then at the nurse.

'Coates?' he said, eventually. 'It says on my form that his name is Archie Duffen . . .'

'I cannot believe it!' A small man with a moustache was pacing up and down behind his desk. 'I still cannot believe a mistake like this could happen in my hospital!'

On the other side of the desk, Cyd and Archie were sitting on a large sofa, with a table in front of them laid with plates of sandwiches, packets of crisps and a selection of cans of drink.

'Never mind,' said Archie. 'These things happen.'

He was dressed in his clothes again now – all except for his socks, which no one had been able to find – and the medicine had not entirely worn off.

'What *did* happen exactly?' asked Cyd.

'You may well ask,' said the man with the
moustache. 'It seems that Archie Duffen, who
is about the same age as Archie here, was
brought in last night complaining of pains in
his head. We took some X-rays, found a blood
clot and realized he needed an operation. He
was supposed to have it this morning.'

'So why wasn't he in his room?' asked Cyd.

'He'd been sent down for some more

X-rays,' the man with the moustache explained. 'And he should have been back, but unfortunately the porter who was sent to get him slipped on a pool of water in the corridor, and had to be taken in for treatment himself. In the meantime, of course, a trainee nurse had put your Archie into his room, and when the nurse came in to give the other Archie his medicine – she'd only just come on duty – she naturally assumed that Archie was, well, Archie . . .'

'Simple mistake,' said Archie, helping himself to another sandwich. 'Could have happened to anyone.'

'It's very nice of you to say so,' said the man with the moustache, 'and I do appreciate it. I just wish there was something I could do to make it up to you.'

Archie was about to say that there was no need, when Cyd spoke for him.

'As a matter of fact,' she said. 'There is one thing . . .'

Later, when Cyd and Archie were walking home, Cyd got a text on her mobile.

'It's all sorted,' she told Archie, when she'd read it. 'Miss Jensen says they've looked at her tests and worked out her medicine, so she's going home this afternoon and she'll be back in school on Monday!'

'That's good,' said Archie.

'And Mum says she's heard from one of her doctor friends that the other Archie had his operation and it all went very well.' Cyd thought for a moment. 'Perhaps we should go and visit him some time.'

'You can go,' said Archie. 'I'm going to stay away from hospitals for a bit.'

Cyd agreed that might be best. 'Though things don't seem to have turned out too badly, do they?' she added. 'I mean, nobody got hurt and . . . well, everyone's happy!'

And Archie had to agree that everyone *was* happy – except his mother when he got home.

'How is it possible,' she demanded, 'to lose *both* socks, just visiting someone in hospital?'

She stomped off upstairs to find him a new pair.

'Honestly! I don't believe it, Archie!'

7. On Sunday...

On Sunday, Archie decided he would like to do something special for his friend, Cyd.

He had been thinking about what had happened the day before, and the more he thought, the more he realized that things could have turned out very differently at the hospital if Cyd had not been there.

Cyd was usually there to help when odd things happened to him, Archie thought. She was the one who had warned him not to pick up the Brazilian Wandering Spider. She had come to the rescue when he was stuck in the staff cloakroom without any clothes. And she was the one who put out the fire in Miss Henley's handbag, so that they hadn't burned to death in the stockroom.

He would like, Archie decided, to do something that showed Cyd how grateful he was for all she had done.

But what?

He was still trying to think of something when his mother appeared.

'Are you ready?' she asked.

'Ready?'

'I thought we'd get down to the station a bit early,' said his mother, 'in case there's a rush.'

And suddenly Archie had the answer.

Three weeks before, his mother had bought two tickets for a trip on the *Tornado*, the first steam train to be built in Britain for more than fifty years. Archie had always loved steam trains and his mother had bought the tickets as an early birthday treat.

Cyd would *love* a trip on a steam train!

'Would you mind,' said Archie, 'if I went on the train with someone else?

'Someone else?' His mother looked slightly hurt. 'You want to go with someone else?'

'I'd like to go with Cyd,' said Archie. 'If you don't mind.'

'Mind?' His mother gave a little sniff. 'Why should I mind? Why should I care if my only son doesn't want to share his birthday treat with me. No, no, I don't mind at all!'

'That's all right, then!' said Archie. 'Thanks, Mum!'

With the train tickets tucked in his pocket, Archie walked straight round to Cyd's house. He didn't tell her where they would be going, he simply said he had a surprise for her.

'Great!' Cyd grabbed her coat. 'I love surprises!'

It should have taken about ten minutes to walk down to the station, but several things happened that meant it took a bit longer than that.

The first thing was that Cyd's hat blew off in the wind, only a few minutes after they'd set out, and a sudden gust lifted it up into the back of a large removal van parked by the pavement.

Cyd climbed into the van to get it back, but her hat had landed on a piece of furniture that was too high for her to reach, so Archie climbed in as well.

He had just rescued the hat, when another
gust of wind blew the door of the van closed
and they were plunged into total darkness.

'Here we go again!' said Cyd, cheerfully. 'I'll bet we can't open the door, and get driven all the way to Scotland or something before they find us!'

'As a matter of fact,' said Archie, 'that happened to me once. I got stuck in a laundry basket and the—'

But Archie never got to say what happened to him in the laundry basket, because at that moment the door at the back of the van opened, to reveal the figure of a woman.

'I don't believe it!' said the woman. 'Archie? Cyd? What are you doing in here?'

The woman standing in

the road was Miss Humber, the teacher who had saved Archie's life on Tuesday by grabbing the spider from his back.

Archie explained about Cyd losing her hat and the doors closing behind them in the wind.

'Well, it's just as well I found you,' Miss Humber chuckled, 'or you might have been stuck in there till we got to Scotland!'

'You're moving to Scotland?' said Cyd.

'I've been offered a job there,' said Miss Humber, 'as a teacher in the village where I grew up. It's what I've always wanted, and I still can't believe how lucky I am!' She smiled. 'It's all thanks to Archie, of course!'

'To me?' said Archie.

'The headmaster of the school I'm going to, saw in the paper about my getting a medal for what I did with the spider,' explained Miss Humber, 'and he wrote and said I was just the sort of person he needed.' She paused. 'How about you both come inside for a drink and a biscuit, and I'll tell you all about it?'

'That's very kind,' said Archie, 'but we don't really have time.'

'Archie's taking me somewhere,' said Cyd. 'For a surprise.'

'Oh, is he!' said Miss Humber, smiling again. 'Well, if Archie's arranged it, I'm sure it'll be something very wonderful!'

Looking at his watch, Archie knew they would have to hurry if they were going to get to the station in time, but when they turned the corner at the end of the road, they found the pavement blocked by a crowd of people gathered outside the church, all trying to take photographs of a couple who had just got married.

Archie and Cyd crossed the road to try and get past, but were stopped by a loud shout.

'I don't believe it!' said a voice. 'It's Archie and Cyd!'

And that was when they realized that the two people getting married were Miss Henley, who had been trapped in the stockroom with them on Wednesday, and Gary, the man who had come to their rescue.

'These are the children I was telling you about!' said Miss Henley, addressing the crowd. 'If it weren't for them, Gary and I would never have found each other again, and we wouldn't be getting married today!'

Everybody gathered round Archie and Cyd, wanting to hear the story, and then

Gary insisted that they be included in the photographs and it was several minutes before Archie was able to say that, much as he would like to stay, they needed to get on.

'Archie's taking me somewhere,' said Cyd, happily. 'For a surprise!'

'A surprise!' Gary beamed down at her. 'Well, I hope it's a nice one!'

'If Archie's arranging it,' said Miss Henley, 'I'm sure it'll be the best surprise ever.'

As they continued their walk to the station, Archie was a little worried that if anything else happened, there might be no surprise at all, and he was very relieved when they got to the station with two minutes to spare.

The entrance to the railway station had glass doors that opened as you went towards them and closed after you'd gone through. Archie was leading the way and the doors opened as he walked towards them, but then started closing again while he was still going through. Before he knew it, they had slammed together on the backpack he was carrying and refused to budge.

'I don't believe it! Not again!' The ticket collector came hurrying towards him. 'That's the second time it's done that this morning!'

Outside, Cyd was trying to pull the doors apart.

'You'll never shift them,' said the railway man, 'not unless you're a professional weight-lifter. You'll have to wait while I phone for the engineer.'

The man disappeared through a door at the side of the ticket hall and Archie waited, trapped in the doorway. There was a clock on the wall in front of him, and it said the *Tornado* was due to depart in exactly one minute.

'Archie?' said a voice. 'Is that you?'

Archie didn't recognize the speaker at first – it was a big woman in yellow shorts and a Hawaiian shirt – but then he saw the tattoo around her neck. It was Miss Hurrell, the teacher who, on Monday, had thought he wanted to kill her, thrown him onto his back in the corridor, and sat on him.

'Are you all right?' she asked.

'He's trapped in the doors,' said Cyd, 'and we can't open them.'

'Well, I might be able to help you there,' said Miss Hurrell. She briefly flexed her fingers, reached out, grabbed a door in each hand and . . . heaved.

There was grinding noise and the doors moved slowly apart. Archie stepped forward,

and Cyd followed him through.

'You are incredible, Miss Hurrell!' she said. 'Thank you! Thank you *so* much!'

'I'm glad I could help,' said Miss Hurrell. 'As a matter of fact, I was hoping for a chance to say thank you to Archie. It's because of him that I've got back into professional wrestling. I don't know if you heard, but I've got this contract in America and—'

'Would you mind,' said Archie, 'if we heard about it some other time?'

'We have to hurry,' said Cyd. 'Archie's got a surprise for me!'

'A surprise?' Miss Hurrell chuckled. 'Well, he's good at those, isn't he? Go on, go for it!'

Shouting thank you and goodbye as they went, Archie started running, and Cyd followed him.

They ran past the ticket office, across the station lobby, along the bridge and then down the stairs that led to the platform. Archie was jumping the stairs two at a time when, halfway down, there was the *toot toot* of a steam whistle and . . .

. . . and ahead of him he could see the

Tornado, in a thunder of steam and noise, pulling gracefully away from the station, to the sound of cheers from the watching crowds.

Archie stopped, his head falling on to his chest in disappointment. That was it. They had missed the train. There would be no surprise for Cyd.

Sadly, he turned to his friend to say how sorry he was, but found she was not looking at the departing steam train. Instead, she was looking at the other platform where a diesel with three coaches had just pulled in. That platform was almost empty, but Cyd was staring at it, frozen to the spot.

'I don't believe it,' she murmured. 'I don't *believe* it!'

With the clouds of steam from the departing *Tornado* still swirling round the platform, Archie couldn't see what she was looking at, but then the clouds parted and he could make out the tall figure of a man in army uniform, adjusting the cap on his head, before picking up a kit bag and slinging it over his shoulder.

'Daddy!' Cyd's voice echoed round the station. 'It's my *daddy*!'

Even as she spoke, she was jumping down the last few steps and racing along the platform as fast as her legs could carry her. And then the man in the uniform saw her and his face broke into the biggest smile Archie had ever seen, and as Cyd came flying towards him he dropped the kit bag, held out his arms and caught her, and held her, and swung her round . . .

. . . and round . . .

. . . and round.

Archie watched from the bottom of the

stairs as the man eventually lowered Cyd to the ground, and then he waited as the two of them slowly made their way back towards him.

'This is Archie,' said Cyd to her father. 'He told me he had a surprise for me, but I never imagined it'd be this. I still can't believe it!'

'Neither can I,' said her father. He turned to Archie. 'I didn't think anyone knew I was coming. I didn't know myself till this morning. How did you find out?'

'Well . . .' Archie wasn't quite sure what to say.

'Nobody knows how Archie does these things,' Cyd answered for him. 'They just happen.'

'Do they . . .' Cyd's father looked down at Archie and his eyes twinkled. 'You sound like a good sort of friend to have, Archie!'

'He's the *best* friend to have,' said Cyd firmly. 'The *very* best!'

Archie walked back from the station alone. Cyd and her dad had taken a taxi to go and see Cyd's mother at work. They had asked Archie if he'd like to come with them, but he had said no thank you. He had a feeling that Cyd and her father might like a bit of time alone together.

Things had not gone quite as he had planned, he thought, as he walked up the path to his front door, but they seemed to have turned out all right. He might have missed his ride on a steam train, but it had been worth it, to see Cyd and her father so happy.

His mother, however, was not at all happy when she saw him.

'All the trouble I went to getting those tickets,' she said. 'And first you tell me not to come with you, and then you don't even bother to use them!'

'Honestly!' She turned on her heels. 'I don't believe it, Archie!'